BOBOK

FROM SOMEBODY'S DIARY

BY

FYODOR DOSTOEVSKY

First Published in 1873

British Library Cataloguing-in-Publication Data
A catalogue record for this book is available
from the British Library

CONTENTS

FYODOR DOSTOEVSKY

Fyodor Mikhailovich Dostoevsky was born in Moscow, as the second son of a former army doctor. Raised within the grounds of the Mariinsky hospital, at an early age he was introduced to English, French, German and Russian literature, as well as to fairy-tales and legends. He was educated at home and at a private school, but shortly after the death of his mother in 1837, he was sent to St. Petersburg, where he entered the Army Engineering College.

In 1839 Dostoevsky's father died. A year later, Dostoevsky graduated as a military engineer, but resigned in 1844 to devote himself to writing. While earning money from translations, he wrote his first novel, *Poor Folk,* which appeared in 1846. It was followed by *The Double* (1846), which depicted a man who was haunted by a look-alike who eventually usurps his position.

In 1846, Dostoevsky joined a group of utopian socialists. He was arrested in 1849 and sentenced to death. After a mock execution, his sentence was reduced to imprisonment in Siberia. Dostoevsky spent four years in hard labour – ten years later, he would turn these experiences into *The House of the Dead* (1860). Upon his release, he joined the army in Semipalatinsk (North-East Kazakhstan), where he remained for a further four years.

Dostoevsky returned to St. Petersburg in 1854. Three years later, he married Maria Isaev, a 29-year old widow. He resigned from the army in 1859, and focussed once more on writing. Between the years 1861 and 1863 he served as editor of the monthly periodical *Time*, which was later suppressed because of an article on the Polish uprising.

In 1864-65 his wife and brother died and Dostoevsky was burdened with debts. The situation was made worse by his own lifelong gambling addiction. From the turmoil of the 1860s emerged his classic *Notes from the Underground* (1864), a psychological study of a social outcast seeking spiritual rebirth. The novel marked a watershed in Dostoevsky's artistic development.

Notes from the Underground (1864) was followed by Dostoevsky's most famous work, *Crime and Punishment* (1866). An account of an individual's fall and redemption, and an implicit critique of nihilism, it is now regarded as one of the greatest works of Russian literature. Two years later *The Idiot* (1868) was published, and three years after that came *The Possessed*, (1871) an exploration of philosophical nihilism.

In 1867 Dostoevsky married Anna Snitkin, his 22-year old stenographer. They travelled abroad and returned in 1871. By the time the *The Brothers Karamazov* was published, between 1879-80, Dostoevsky was recognized in his own country as one of its great writers. However, having suffered from a fragile mental disposition his whole life, Dostoevsky began to succumb to larger periods of mania and rage. After a particularly bad epileptic fit, he died in St. Petersburg in early 1881, aged 59.

Together with Leo Tolstoy, Dostoevsky is now regarded as one of the greatest and most influential novelists in all of Russian literature. His books have been translated into more than 170 languages and have sold around 15 million copies.

BOBOK

[A Bobok is a small bean]

Semyon Ardalyonovitch said to me all of a sudden the day before yesterday: "Why, will you ever be sober, Ivan Ivanovitch? Tell me that, pray."

A strange requirement. I did not resent it, I am a timid man; but here they have actually made me out mad. An artist painted my portrait as it happened: "After all, you are a literary man," he said. I submitted, he exhibited it. I read: "Go and look at that morbid face suggesting insanity."

It may be so, but think of putting it so bluntly into print. In print everything ought to be decorous; there ought to be ideals, while instead of that . . .

Say it indirectly, at least; that's what you have style for. But no, he doesn't care to do it indirectly. Nowadays humour and a fine style have disappeared, and abuse is accepted as wit. I do not resent it: but God knows I am not enough of a literary man to go out of my mind. I have written a novel, it has not been published. I have written articles — they have been refused. Those articles I took about from one editor to another; everywhere they refused them: you have no salt they told me. "What sort of salt do you want?" I asked with a eer. "Attic salt?"

They did not even understand, For the most part I translate from the French for the booksellers. I write advertisements for shopkeepers too: "Unique opportunity! Fine tea, from our own plantations . . ." I made a nice little sum over a panegyric on his deceased excellency Pyotr Matveyitch. I compiled the "Art of pleasing the ladies", a commission from a bookseller. I have brought out some six little works of this kind in the course of my life. I am thinking of making a collection of the bons mobs of Voltaire, but am afraid it may seem a little flat to our people. Voltaire's no good now; nowadays we want a cudgel, not Voltaire. We knock each other's last teeth out nowadays. Well, so that's the whole extent of my literary activity. Though indeed I do send round letters to the editors gratis and fully signed. I give them all sorts of counsels and admonitions, criticise and point out the true path. The letter I sent last week to an editor's office was the fortieth I had sent in the last two years. I have wasted four roubles over stamps alone for them. My temper is at the bottom of it all.

I believe that the artist who painted me did so not for the sake of literature, but for the sake of two symmetrical warts on my forehead, a natural phenomenon, he would say. They have no ideas, so now they are out for phenomena. And didn't he succeed in getting my warts in his portrait — to the life. That is what they call realism.

And as to madness, a great many people were put down as mad among us last year. And in such language! "With such original talent . . . . and yet, after all, it appears" . . . "however, one ought to have foreseen it long ago." That is rather artful; so that from the point of view of pure art one may really commend it. Well, but after all, these so-called madmen have turned out cleverer than ever. So it seems the critics can call them mad, but they cannot produce anyone better.

The wisest of all, in my opinion, is he who can, if only once a month, call himself a fool — a faculty unheard of nowadays. In old days, once a year at any rate a fool would recognise that he was a fool, but nowadays not a bit of it. And they have so muddled things up that there is no telling a fool from a wise man. They have done that on purpose.

I remember a witty Spaniard saying when, two hundred and fifty years ago, the French built their first madhouses: "They have shut up all their fools in a house apart, to make sure that they are wise men themselves." Just so: you don't show your own wisdom by shutting someone else in a madhouse. "K. has gone out of his mind, means that we are sane now." No, it doesn't mean that yet.

Hang it though, why am I maundering on? I go on grumbling and grumbling. Even my maidservant is sick of me. Yesterday a friend came to see me. "Your style is changing," he said; "it is choppy: you chop and chop — and then a parenthesis, then a parenthesis in the parenthesis, then you stick in something else in brackets, then you begin chopping and chopping again."

The friend is right. Something strange is happening to me. My character is changing and my head aches. I am beginning to see and hear strange things, not voices exactly, but as though someone beside me were muttering, "bobok, bobok, bobok!"

What's the meaning of this bobok? I must divert my mind.

I went out in search of diversion, I hit upon a funeral. A distant relation — a collegiate counsellor, however. A widow and five daughters, all marriageable young ladies. What must it come to even to keep them in slippers. Their father managed it, but now there is only a little pension. They will have to eat humble pie. They have always received me ungraciously. And indeed I should not have gone to the funeral now had it not been for a peculiar circumstance. I followed the procession to the cemetery with the rest; they were stuck-up and held aloof from me. My uniform was certainly rather shabby. It's five-and-twenty years, I believe, since I was at the cemetery; what a wretched place!

To begin with the smell. There were fifteen hearses, with palls varying in expensiveness; there were actually two catafalques. One was a general's and one some lady's. There were many mourners, a great deal of feigned mourning and a great deal of open gaiety. The clergy have nothing to complain of; it brings them a good income. But the smell, the smell. I should not like to be one of the clergy here.

I kept glancing at the faces of the dead cautiously, distrusting my impressionability. Some had a mild expression, some looked unpleasant. As a rule the smiles were disagreeable, and in some cases very much so. I don't like them; they haunt one's dreams.

During the service I went out of the church into the air: it was a grey day, but dry. It was cold too, but then it was October. I walked about among the tombs. They are of different grades. The third grade cost thirty roubles; it's decent and not so very dear. The first two grades are tombs in the church and under the porch; they cost a pretty penny. On this occasion they were burying in tombs of the third grade six persons, among them the general and the lady.

I looked into the graves — and it was horrible: water and such water! Absolutely green, and . . . but there, why talk of it! The gravedigger was baling it out every minute. I went out while the service was going on and strolled outside the gates. Close by was an almshouse, and a little further off there was a restaurant. It was not a bad little restaurant: there was lunch and everything. There were lots of the mourners here. I noticed a great deal of gaiety and genuine heartiness. I had something to eat and drink.

Then I took part in the bearing of the coffin from the church to the grave. Why is it that corpses in their coffins are so heavy? They say it is due to some sort of inertia, that the body is no longer directed by its owner . . . or some nonsense of that sort, in opposition to the laws of mechanics and common sense. I don't like to hear people who have nothing but a general education venture to solve the problems that require special knowledge; and with us that's done continually. Civilians love to pass opinions about subjects that are the province of the soldier and even of the field-marshal; while men who have been educated as engineers prefer discussing philosophy and political economy.

I did not go to the requiem service. I have some pride, and if I am only received owing to some special necessity, why force myself on their dinners, even if it be a funeral dinner. The only thing I don't understand is why I stayed at the cemetery; I sat on a tombstone and sank into appropriate reflections.

I began with the Moscow exhibition and ended with reflecting upon astonishment in the abstract. My deductions about astonishment were these:

"To be surprised at everything is stupid of course, and to be astonished at nothing is a great deal more becoming and for some reason accepted as good form. But that is not really true. To my mind to be astonished at nothing is much more stupid than to be astonished at everything. And, moreover, to be astonished at nothing is almost the same as feeling respect for nothing. And indeed a stupid man is incapable of feeling respect."

"But what I desire most of all is to feel respect. I thirst to feel respect," one of my acquaintances said to me the other day.

He thirsts to feel respect! Goodness, I thought, what would happen to you if you dared to print that nowadays? At that point I sank into forgetfulness. I don't like reading the epitaphs of tombstones: they are everlastingly the same. An unfinished sandwich was lying on the tombstone near me; stupid and inappropriate. I threw it on the ground, as it was not bread but only a sandwich. Though I believe it is not a sin to throw bread on the earth, but only on the floor. I must look it up in Suvorin's calendar.

I suppose I sat there a long time-too long a time, in fact; I must have lain down on a long stone which was of the shape of a marble coffin. And how it happened I don't know, but I began to hear things of all sorts being said. At first I did not pay attention to it, but treated it with contempt. But the conversation went on. I heard muffled sounds as though the speakers' mouths were covered with a pillow, and at the same time they were distinct and very near. I came to myself, sat up and began listening attentively.

"Your Excellency, it's utterly impossible. You led hearts, I return your lead, and here you play the seven of diamonds. You ought to have given me a hint about diamonds."

"What, play by hard and fast rules? Where is the charm of that?"

"You must, your Excellency. One can't do anything without something to go upon. We must play with dummy, let one hand not be turned up."

"Well, you won't find a dummy here."

What conceited words! And it was queer and unexpected. One was such a ponderous, dignified voice, the other softly suave; I should not have believed it if I had not heard it myself. I had not been to the requiem dinner, I believe. And yet how could they be playing preference here and what general was this? That the sounds came from under the tombstones of that there could be no doubt. I bent down and read on the tomb:

"Here lies the body of Major-General Pervoyedov . . . a cavalier of such and such orders." Hm! "Passed away in August of this year . . . fifty-seven. . . . Rest, beloved ashes, till the joyful dawn!"

Hm, dash it, it really is a general! There was no monument on the grave from which the obsequious voice came, there was only a tombstone. He must have been a fresh arrival. From his voice he was a lower court councillor.

"Oh-ho-ho-ho!" I heard in a new voice a dozen yards from the general's resting-place, coming from quite a fresh grave. The voice belonged to a man and a plebeian, mawkish with its affectation of religious fervour. "Oh-ho-ho-ho!"

"Oh, here he is hiccupping again!" cried the haughty and disdainful voice of an irritated lady, apparently of the highest society. "It is an affliction to be by this shopkeeper!"

"I didn't hiccup; why, I've had nothing to eat. It's simply my nature. Really, madam, you don't seem able to get rid of your caprices here."

"Then why did you come and lie down here?"

"They put me here, my wife and little children put me here, I did not lie down here of myself. The mystery of death! And I would not have lain down beside you not for any money; I lie here as befitting my fortune, judging by the price. For we can always do that — pay for a tomb of the third grade."

"You made money, I suppose? You fleeced people?"

"Fleece you, indeed! We haven't seen the colour of your money since January. There's a little bill against you at the shop."

"Well, that's really stupid; to try and recover debts here is too stupid, to my thinking! Go to the surface. Ask my niece — she is my heiress."

"There's no asking anyone now, and no going anywhere. We have both reached our limit and, before the judgment-seat of God, are equal in our sins."

"In our sins," the lady mimicked him contemptuously. "Don't dare to speak to me."

"Oh-ho-ho-ho!"

"You see, the shopkeeper obeys the lady, your Excellency."

"Why shouldn't he?"

"Why, your Excellency, because, as we all know, things are different here."

"Different? How?"

"We are dead, so to speak, your Excellency."

"Oh, yes! But still . . ."

Well, this is an entertainment, it is a fine show, I must say! If it has come to this down here, what can one expect on the surface? But what a queer business! I went on listening, however, though with extreme indignation.

"Yes, I should like a taste of life! Yes, you know . . . I should like a taste of fife." I heard a new voice suddenly somewhere in the space between the general and the irritable lady.

"Do you hear, your Excellency, our friend is at the same game again. For three days at a time he says nothing, and then he bursts out with 'I should like a taste of life, yes, a taste of life!' And with such appetite, he-he!"

"And such frivolity."

"It gets hold of him, your Excellency, and do you know, he is growing sleepy, quite sleepy — he has been here since April; and then all of a sudden 'I should like a taste of life!'"

"It is rather dull, though," observed his Excellency.

"It is, your Excellency. Shall we tease Avdotya Ignatyevna again, he-he?"

"No, spare me, please. I can't endure that quarrelsome virago."

"And I can't endure either of you," cried the virago disdainfully. "You are both of you bores and can't tell me anything ideal. I know one little story about you, your Excellency — don't turn up your nose, please — how a manservant swept you out from under a married couple's bed one morning."

"Nasty woman," the general muttered through his teeth.

"Avdotya lgnatycvna, ma'am," the shopkeeper wailed suddenly again, "my dear lady, don't be angry, but tell me, am I going through the ordeal by torment now, or is it something else?"

"Ah, he is at it again, as I expected! For there's a smell from him which means he is turning round!"

"I am not turning round, ma'am, and there's no particular smell from me, for I've kept my body whole as it should be, while you're regularly high. For the smell is really horrible even for a place like this. I don't speak of it, merely from politeness."

"Ah, you horrid, insulting wretch. He positively stinks and talks about me."

"Oh-ho-ho-ho! If only the time for my requiem would come quickly: I should hear their tearful voices over my head, my wife's lament and my children's soft weeping! . . ."

"Well, that's a thing to fret for! They'll stuff themselves with funeral rice and go home. . . . Oh, I wish somebody would wake up!"

"Avdotya Ignatyevna," said the insinuating government clerk, "wait a bit, the new arrivals will speak."

"And are there any young people among them?"

"Yes, there are, Avdotya lgnatyevna. There are some not more than lads."

"Oh, how welcome that would be!"

"Haven't they begun yet?" inquired his Excellency.

"Even those who came the day before yesterday haven't awakened yet, your Excellency. As you know, they sometimes don't speak for a week. It's a good job that to-day and yesterday and the day before they brought a whole lot. As it is, they are all last year's for seventy feet round."

"Yes, it will be interesting."

"Yes, your Excellency, they buried Tarasevitch, the privy councillor, to-day. I knew it from the voices. I know his nephew, he helped to lower the coffin just now."

"Hm, where is he, then?"

"Five steps from you, your Excellency, on the left. . . . Almost at your feet. You should make his acquaintance, your Excellency."

"Hm, no — it's not for me to make advances."

"Oh, he will begin of himself, your Excellency. He will be flattered. Leave it to me, your Excellency, and I . . ."

"Oh, oh! . . . What is happening to me?" croaked the frightened voice of a new arrival.

"A new arrival, your Excellency, a new arrival, thank God! And how quick he's been! Sometimes they don't say a word for a week."

"Oh, I believe it's a young man!" Avdotya Ignatyevna cried shrilly.

"I . . . I . . . it was a complication, and so sudden!" faltered the young man again. "Only the evening before, Schultz said to me, 'There's a complication,' and I died suddenly before morning. Oh! oh!"

"Well, there's no help for it, young man," the general observed graciously, evidently pleased at a new arrival. "You must be comforted. You are kindly welcome to our Vale of Jehoshaphat, so to call it. We are kind-hearted people, you will come to know us and appreciate us. Major-General Vassili Vassilitch Pervoyedov, at your service."

"Oh, no, no! Certainly not! I was at Schultz's; I had a complication, you know, at first it was my chest and a cough, and then I caught a cold: my lungs and influenza . . . and all of a sudden, quite unexpectedly . . . the worst of all was its being so unexpected."

"You say it began with the chest," the government clerk put in suavely, as though he wished to reassure the new arrival.

"Yes, my chest and catarrh and then no catarrh, but still the chest, and I couldn't breathe . . . and you know . . . "

"I know, I know. But if it was the chest you ought to have gone to Ecke and not to Schultz."

"You know, I kept meaning to go to Botkin's, and all at once . . ."

"Botkin is quite prohibitive," observed the general.

"Oh, no, he is not forbidding at all; I've heard he is so attentive and foretells everything beforehand."

"His Excellency was referring to his fees," the government clerk corrected him.

"Oh, not at all, he only asks three roubles, and he makes such an examination, and gives you a prescription . . . and I was very anxious to see him, for I have been told . . . Well, gentlemen, had I better go to Ecke or to Botkin?"

"What? To whom?" The general's corpse shook with agreeable laughter. The government clerk echoed it in falsetto.

"Dear boy, dear, delightful boy, how I love you!" Avdotya Ignatyevna squealed ecstatically. "I wish they had put someone like you next to me."

No, that was too much! And these were the dead of our times! Still, I ought to listen to more and not be in too great a hurry to draw conclusions. That snivelling new arrival — I remember him just now in his coffin — had the expression of a frightened chicken, the most revolting expression in the world! However, let us wait and see.

But what happened next was such a Bedlam that I could not keep it all in my memory. For a great many woke up at once; an official — a civil councillor — woke up, and began discussing at once the project of a new sub-committee in a government department and of the probable transfer of various functionaries in connection with the sub-committee — which very greatly interested the general. I must confess I learnt a great deal that was new myself, so much so that I marvelled at the channels by which one may sometimes in the metropolis learn government news. Then an engineer half woke up, but for a long time muttered absolute nonsense, so that our friends left off worrying him and let him lie till he was ready. At last the distinguished lady who had been buried in the morning under the catafalque showed symptoms of the reanimation of the tomb. Lebeziatnikov (for the obsequious lower court councillor whom I detested and who lay beside General Pervoyedov was called, it appears, Lebeziatnikov) became much excited, and surprised that they were all waking up so soon tllis time. I must own I was surprised too; though some of those who woke had been buried for three days, as, for instance, a very young girl of sixteen who kept giggling . . . giggling in a horrible and predatory way.

"Your Excellency, privy councillor Tarasevitch is waking!" Lebeziatnikov announced with extreme fussiness.

"Eh? What?" the privy councillor, waking up suddenly mumbled, with a lisp of disgust. There was a note of ill-humoured peremptoriness in the sound of his voice.

I listened with curiosity — for during the last few days I had heard something about Tarasevitch — shocking and upsetting in the extreme.

"It's I, your Excellency, so far only I."

"What is your petition? What do you want?"

"Merely to inquire after your Excellency's health; in these unaccustomed surroundings everyone feels at first, as it were, oppressed. General Pervoyedov wishes to have the honour of making your Excellency's acquaintance, and hopes . . ."

"I've never heard of him."

"Surely, your Excellency! General Pervoyedov, Vassili Vassilitch . . ."

"Are you General Pervoyedov?"

"No, your Excellency, I am only the lower court councillor Lebeziatnikov, at your service, but General Pervoyedov . . ."

"Nonsense! And I beg you to leave me alone."

"Let him be." General Pervoyedov at last himself checked with dignity the disgusting officiousness of his sycophant in the grave.

"He is not fully awake, your Excellency, you must consider

that; it's the novelty of it all. When he is fully awake he will take it differently."

"Let him be," repeated the general.

"Vassili Vassilitch! Hey, your Excellency!" a perfectly new voice shouted loudly and aggressively from close beside Avdotya lgnatyevna. It was a voice of gentlemanly insolence, with the languid pronunciation now fashionable and an arrogant drawl. "I've been watching you all for the last two hours. Do you remember me, Vassili Vassilitch? My name is Klinevitch, we met at the Volokonskys' where you, too, were received as a guest, I am sure I don't know why."

"What, Count Pyotr Petrovitch? . . . Can it be really you . . . and at such an early age? How sorry I am to hear it."

"Oh, I am sorry myself, though I really don't mind, and I want to amuse myself as far as I can everywhere. And I am not a count but a baron, only a baron. We are only a set of scurvy barons, risen from being flunkeys, but why I don't know and I don't care. I am only a scoundrel of the pseudo-aristocratic society, and I am regarded as 'a charming polisson'. My father is a wretched little general, and my mother was at one time received en haut lieu. With the help of the Jew Zifel I forged fifty thousand rouble notes last year and then I informed against him, while Julic Charpentier de Lusignan carried off the money to Bordeaux. And only fancy, I was engaged to be married — to a girl still at school, three months under sixteen, with a dowry of ninety thousand. Avdotya lgnatyevna, do you remember how you seduced me fifteen years ago when I was a boy of fourteen in the Corps des Pages?"

"Ah, that's you, you rascal! Well, you are a godsend, anyway, for here . . . ."

"You were mistaken in suspecting your neighbour, the business gentleman, of unpleasant fragrance. . . . I said nothing, but I laughed. The stench came from me: they had to bury me in a nailed-up coffin."

"Ugh, you horrid creature! Still, I am glad you are here; you can't imagine the lack of life and wit here."

"Quite so, quite so, and I intend to start here something original. Your Excellency — I don't mean you, Pervoyedov — your Excellency the other one, Tarasevitch, the privy councillor! Answer! I am Klinevitch, who took you to Mlle. Furie in Lent, do you hear?"

"I do, Klinevitch, and I am delighted, and trust me ."

"I wouldn't trust you with a halfpenny, and I don't care. I simply want to kiss you, dear old man, but luckily I can't. Do you know, gentlemen, what this grand-pere's little game was? He died three or four days ago, and would you believe it, he left a deficit of four hundred thousand government money from the fund for widows and orphans. He was the sole person in control of it for some reason, so that his accounts were not audited for the last eight years. I can fancy what long faces they all have now, and what they call him. It's a delectable thought, isn't it? I have been wondering for the last year how a wretched old man of seventy, gouty and rheumatic, succeeded in preserving the physical energy for his debaucheries — and now the riddle is solved! Those widows and orphans — the very thought of them must have egged him on! I knew about it long ago, I was the only one who did know; it was Julie told me, and as soon as I discovered it, I attacked him in a friendly way at once in Easter week: 'Give me twenty-five thousand, if you don't they'll look into your accounts to-morrow.' And just fancy, he had only thirteen thousand left then, so it seems it was very apropos his dying now. Grand-pere, grand-pere; do you hear?"

"Cher Khnevitch, I quite agree with you, and there was no need for you . . . to go into such details. Life is so full of suffering and torment and so little to make up for it . . . that I wanted at last to be at rest, and so far as I can see I hope to get all I can from here too."

"I bet that he has already sniffed Katiche Berestoy!"

"Who? What Katiche?" There was a rapacious quiver in the old man's voice.

"A-ah, what Katiche? Why, here on the left, five paces from

me and ten from you. She has been here for five days, and if only you knew, grand-pere, what a little wretch she is! Of good family and breeding and a monster, a regular monster! I did not introduce her to anyone there, I was the only one who knew her. ... Katiche, answer!"

"He-he-he!" the girl responded with a jangling laugh, in which there was a note of something as sharp as the prick of a needle. "He-he-he!"

"And a little blonde?" the grand-pere faltered, drawling out the syllables.

"He-he-he!"

"I ... have long ... I have long," the old man faltered breathlessly, "cherished the dream of a little fair thing of fifteen and just in such surroundings."

"Ach, the monster!" cried Avdotya Ignatyevna.

"Enough!" Klinevitch decided. "I see there is excellent material. We shall soon arrange things better. The great thing is to spend the rest of our time cheerfully; but what time? Hey, you, government clerk, Lebeziatnikov or whatever it is, I hear that's your name!"

"Semyon Yevseitch Lebeziatnikov, lower court councillor, at your service, very, very, very much delighted to meet you."

"I don't care whether you are delighted or not, but you seem to know everything here. Tell me first of all how it is we can talk? I've been wondering ever since yesterday. We are dead and yet we are talking and seem to be moving — and yet we are not talking and not moving. What jugglery is this?"

"If you want an explanation, baron, Platon Nikolaevitch could give you one better than I."

"What Platon Nikolaevitch is that? To the point. Don't beat about the bush."

"Platon Nikolaevitch is our home-grown philosopher, scientist and Master of Arts. He has brought out several philosophical works, but for the last three months he has been getting quite drowsy, and there is no stirring him up now. Once a week he

20

mutters something utterly irrelevant."

"To the point, to the point!"

"He explains all this by the simplest fact, namely, that when we were living on the surface we mistakenly thought that death there was death. The body revives, as it were, here, the remains of life are concentrated, but only in consciousness. I don't know how to express it, but life goes on, as it were, by inertia. In his opinion everything is concentrated somewhere in consciousness and goes on for two or three months . . . sometimes even for half a year. . . . There is one here, for instance, who is almost completely decomposed, but once every six weeks he suddenly utters one word, quite senseless of course, about some bobok, 'Bobok, bobok,' but you see that an imperceptible speck of life is still warm within him."

"It's rather stupid. Well, and how is it I have no sense of smell and yet I feel there's a stench?"

"That . . . he-he . . . Well, on that point our philosopher is a bit foggy. It's apropos of smell, he said, that the stench one perceives here is, so to speak, moral — he-he! It's the stench of the soul, he says, that in these two or three months it may have time to recover itself . . . and this is, so to speak, the last mercy. . . . Only, I think, baron, that these are mystic ravings very excusable in his position . . .

"Enough; all the rest of it, I am sure, is nonsense. The great thing is that we have two or three months more of life and then — bobok! I propose to spend these two months as agreeably as possible, and so to arrange everything on a new basis. Gentlemen! I propose to cast aside all shame."

"Ah, let us cast aside all shame, let us!" many voices could be heard saying; and strange to say, several new voices were audible, which must have belonged to others newly awakened. The engineer, now fully awake, boomed out his agreement with peculiar delight. The girl Katiche giggled gleefully.

"Oh, how I long to cast off all shame!" Avdotya lgnatyevna exclaimed rapturously.

"I say, if Avdotya lgnatyevna wants to cast off all shame . . . "

"No, no, no, Klinevitch, I was ashamed up there all the same, but here I should like to cast off shame, I should like it awfully."

"I understand, Klinevitch," boomed the engineer, "that you want to rearrange life here on new and rational principles."

"Oh, I don't care a hang about that! For that we'll wait for Kudeyarov who was brought here yesterday. When he wakes he'll tell you all about it. He is such a personality, such a titanic personality! To-morrow they'll bring along another natural scientist, I believe, an officer for certain, and three or four days later a journalist, and, I believe, his editor with him. But deuce take them all, there will be a little group of us anyway, and things will arrange themselves. Though meanwhile I don't want us to be telling lies. That's all I care about, for that is one thing that matters. One cannot exist on the surface without lying, for life and lying are synonymous, but here we will amuse ourselves by not lying. Hang it all, the grave has some value after all! We'll all tell our stories aloud, and we won't be ashamed of anything. First of all I'll tell you about myself. I am one of the predatory kind, you know. All that was bound and held in check by rotten cords up there on the surface. Away with cords and let us spend these two months in shameless truthfulness! Let us strip and be naked!"

"Let us be naked, let us be naked!" cried all the voices.

"I long to be naked, I long to be," Avdotya Ignatyevna shrilled.

"Ah . . . ah, I see we shall have fun here; I don't want Ecke after all."

"No, I tell you. Give me a taste of life!"

"He-he-he!" giggled Katiche.

"The great thing is that no one can interfere with us, and though I see Pervoyedov is in a temper, he can't reach me with his hand. Grand-pere, do you agree?"

"I fully agree, fully, and with the utmost satisfaction, but on condition that Katiche is the first to give us her biography."

"I protest! I protest with all my heart!" General Pervoyedov brought out firmly.

"Your Excellency!" the scoundrel Lebeziatnikov persuaded him in a murmur of fussy excitement, "your Excellency, it will be to our advantage to agree. Here, you see, there's this girl's . . . and all their little affairs."

"There's the girl, it's true, but . . . "

"It's to our advantage, your Excellency, upon my word it is! If only as an experiment, let us try it. . ."

"Even in the grave they won't let us rest in peace."

"In the first place, General, you were playing preference in the grave, and in the second we don't care a hang about you," drawled Klinevitch.

"Sir, I beg you not to forget yourself."

"What? Why, you can't get at me, and I can tease you from here as though you were Julie's lapdog. And another thing, gentlemen, how is he a general here? He was a general there, but here is mere refuse."

"No, not mere refuse. . . . Even here . . . "

"Here you will rot in the grave and six brass buttons will be all that will be left of you."

"Bravo, Klinevitch, ha-ha-ha!" roared voices.

"I have served my sovereign. . . . I have the sword . . ."

"Your sword is only fit to prick mice, and you never drew it even for that."

"That makes no difference; I formed a part of the whole."

"There are all sorts of parts in a whole."

"Bravo, Klinevitch, bravo! Ha-ha-ha!"

"I don't understand what the sword stands for," boomed the engineer.

"We shall run away from the Prussians like mice, they'll crush us to powder!" cried a voice in the distance that was unfamiliar to me, that was positively spluttering with glee.

"The sword, sir, is an honour," the general cried, but only I heard him. There arose a prolonged and furious roar, clamour, and hubbub, and only the hysterically impatient squeals of Avdotya Ignatyevna were audible.

"But do let us make haste! Ah, when are we going to begin to cast off all shame!"

"Oh-ho-ho! . . . The soul does in truth pass through torments!" exclaimed the voice of the plebeian, "and . . ."

And here I suddenly sneezed. It happened suddenly and unintentionally, but the effect was striking: all became as silent as one expects it to be in a churchyard, it all vanished like a dream. A real silence of the tomb set in. I don't believe they were ashamed on account of my presence: they had made up their minds to cast off all shame! I waited five minutes — not a word, not a sound. It cannot be supposed that they were afraid of my informing the police; for what could the police do to them? I must conclude that they had some secret unknown to the living, which they carefully concealed from every mortal.

"Well, my dears," I thought, "I shall visit you again." And with those words, I left the cemetery.

No, that I cannot admit; no, I really cannot! The bobok case does not trouble me (so that is what the bobok signified!)

Depravity in such a place, depravity of the last aspirations, depravity of sodden and rotten corpses — and not even sparing the last inoments of consciousness! Those moments have been granted, vouchsafed to them, and . . . and, worst of all, in such a place! No, that I cannot admit.

I shall go to other tombs, I shall listen everywhere. Certainly one ought to listen everywhere and not merely at one spot in order to form an idea. Perhaps one may come across something reassuring.

But I shall certainly go back to those. They promised their biographies and anecdotes of all sorts. Tfoo! But I shall go, I shall certainly go; it is a question of conscience!

I shall take it to the Citizen; the editor there has had his portrait exhibited too. Maybe he will print it.

www.ingramcontent.com/pod-product-compliance
Lightning Source LLC
Chambersburg PA
CBHW030137260626
47156CB00008B/2977